# *Tales to* Frighten and Delight

# Also by Pleasant DeSpain

---

THE BOOKS OF NINE LIVES SERIES

VOL. 1: ***Tales of Tricksters***

VOL. 2: ***Tales of Nonsense and Tomfoolery***

VOL. 3: ***Tales of Wisdom and Justice***

VOL. 4: ***Tales of Heroes***

VOL. 5: ***Tales of Holidays***

VOL. 6: ***Tales of Insects***

VOL. 7: ***Tales of Enchantment***

VOL. 8: ***Tales to Frighten and Delight***

VOL. 9: ***Tales of Cats***

---

***The Dancing Turtle***
A Folktale from Brazil

***The Emerald Lizard***
Fifteen Latin American Tales to Tell in English & Spanish

***Sweet Land of Story***
Thirty-Six American Tales to Tell

***Thirty-Three Multicultural Tales to Tell***

***Eleven Turtle Tales***
Adventure Tales from Around the World

THE BOOKS OF NINE LIVES

VOLUME EIGHT

# Tales to Frighten and Delight

## Pleasant DeSpain

Illustrations by Don Bell

August House, Inc.
ATLANTA

Published 2003 by August House, Inc.
Atlanta, Georgia
augusthouse.com.

Printed in the United States of America

10  9  8  7  6  5  4  3  2  1    PB

LIBRARY OF CONGRESS CATALOGING-IN-PUBLICATION DATA

DeSpain, Pleasant.
    Tales to frighten and delight / by Pleasant DeSpain ; illustrations by
Don Bell.
        p.  cm. — (The books of nine lives ; v. 8)
    Includes bibliographic references.
    Contents: The dancing skeleton : Japan—Wait till Axel comes : United
States—The hungry witch : Uruguay—The cat on the Dovrefell : Norway—
The ghost wife : Sioux—Godfather death : Germany—The devil's bridge :
France—The horned women : Ireland—The talking skull : Congo.
    ISBN 978-0-87483-712-4 (HC)
    ISBN 978-0-87483-916-6 (PB)
    1. Supernatural—Folklore.  2. Tales. [1. Supernatural—Folklore.
2. Folklore]  I. Bell, Don, 1935– ill.  II. Title
PZ8.1.D453 Tag 2003
398.27—dc21                                              2003050208

Executive editor: Liz Parkhurst
Project editor: April McGee
Text designer: Liz Lester
Cover and book illustration: Don Bell

The paper used in this publication meets the minimum requirements
of the American National Standard for Information Sciences—
Permanence of Paper for Printed Library Materials, ANSI Z39.48–1984.

AUGUST HOUSE        ATLANTA

for Lori and Lorraine Morton-Feazell
and
Tyler Matthew Morton-Feazell,
sisters and nephew of my heart and soul,
a family blessed

## *Acknowledgments*

I'm fortunate to have genuine friends and colleagues without whose help the continuation of this series would not have been possible. Genuine thanks to:

- Liz and Ted Parkhurst, Publishers
- Don Bell, Illustrator
- April McGee, Project Editor
- Margaret Read MacDonald, Storyteller, Author, Librarian
- Jennifer D. Murphy, Head of the Children's Department, Albany, New York Public Library
- Candace E. Deisley, Youth Services Librarian, Albany, New York Public Library
- Deidre McGrath, Youth Services Librarian, Albany, New York Public Library
- Denver Public Library
- Lakewood, Colorado, Public Library
- Seattle Public Library
- University of Washington Library (Seattle)

# The Books of Nine Lives Series

A good story lives each time it's read and told again. The stories in this series have had many lives over the centuries. My retellings have had several lives in the past twenty-plus years, and I'm pleased to witness their new look and feel. Although The Books of Nine Lives series began with a variety of thematically based, and previously published, multicultural tales, all nine of the stories in this volume are printed here for the first time.

This particular volume takes on its own life. The tales are timeless, ageless, universal, and so very human. They deserve to be read and told again.

I'm profoundly grateful to all the teachers, parents, storytellers, and children who have found these tales worthy of sharing. One story always leads to the next. May these lead you to laughter, wisdom, and delight.

As evolving human beings, we are more alike than we are different, each with a story to tell.

—*Pleasant DeSpain*
*Troy, New York*

# Contents

# Introduction

*From ghoulies and ghosties and*
*long-leggety beasties*
*And things that go bump in the night,*
*Good Lord, deliver us.*

—CORNISH PRAYER

Imaginations of all ages come alive when scary stories are shared. The absence of light creates the dark, just as the absence of dark creates the light. Such is life as reflected in the stories we tell.

During the past thirty years, I've told tales to both young and old audiences thousands of times. Whenever I've asked, "Would you like to hear a scary story?," the reply has been a resounding "Yes!" And why not? The lurking, primeval, and shadowy aspect of our whole selves demands acknowledgement. Stories that frighten and delight fulfill and enlighten that need.

I've shared these tales with young and old and found heightened imagination on the listener's side each time. Skeletons dance, and cats talk. Witches have insatiable hunger, and trolls mistake a polar bear for an enormous white cat. A ghost marries a man, and Godfather Death gives a unique gift to his human godson. The devil himself builds a bridge for a costly fee, and women with horns growing from their heads invade a family's home. And when skulls talk, one should heed the message.

Tales from Japan, the United States, Uruguay, Norway, the Sioux Nation, Germany, France, Ireland, and Africa fill this multicultural collection. Read, enjoy, and tell again.

# The Dancing Skeleton

*Japan*

Once, long ago, two village lads left home to see the world. They were close in age but different in temperament. Taro was honest and hardworking, just as Kishi was a lazy scoundrel. During the next three years, Taro earned a small fortune in buying and selling gold. Kishi, on the other hand, gambled and cheated his way into absolute poverty.

One day Taro decided to return to his village. "Would you like to travel back home with me?" he asked his friend.

"Yes," said Kishi, "but my clothes are no

better than rags. I'll be filled with shame to arrive home looking like a beggar."

"I'll buy you a new kimono and give you traveling money as well. It's safer to travel together on the long road back."

Kishi, pleased with the arrangement, made a good walking companion for the many days required to reach the high mountain pass leading to their village. Then he changed back into his true and evil self. He smashed Taro's head with a rock, stole all his gold, and left him to die.

The murdering thief walked down the mountain to his village alone. He explained that Taro had traveled on to a neighboring country and that he had no desire to return home. The villagers were sad, as everyone loved Taro.

Kishi gambled the stolen gold away during the first two years of his return. He then married a wealthy bride and gambled with her money during the next year. He lost it all. Deciding to run away, he left the village in the middle of the night and climbed the mountain path to the top. Here he rested until daybreak.

That's when he heard the rattle and bang of the skeleton's bones.

"Over here behind the trees, Kishi. It's your old friend Taro. I've been waiting to see you again."

Kishi started to run but wasn't fast enough. The skeleton leapt from behind the trees and grabbed onto the sleeve of Kishi's kimono with a bony hand. "Don't be afraid. I'm just a bunch of bones. I can't hurt you. Besides, it's lonely up here on the mountain-top. I want to travel with you."

"I can't travel with a skeleton," said Kishi in a shaky voice. "People will shun me."

"Not if we amaze and delight them," said the skeleton. "I'll dance in the marketplaces, and you can call the tunes and collect the coins. I have no need of money so you can keep all of it. You'll become famous and make a fortune."

Kishi liked the sound of that. He gathered up the skeleton's many bones and put them in his sack. After walking to a distant village, Kishi poured the bones onto the ground in the middle of the marketplace. He called a tune, and the bones quickly assembled themselves. The skeleton jumped up and began to dance, jerking its legs up and down and waving its long arms in the air. It tossed its head back and forth and forth and back. The dance ended and the skeleton fell down. The people applauded and filled Kishi's straw hat with coins, just as Taro predicted. It wasn't long before Kishi and his dancing skeleton became known throughout the land.

The emperor ordered Kishi and the skeleton to perform in the Imperial Palace during the Autumn Celebration. It was a great

honor, and the hall was filled with a thousand privileged guests. Kishi poured the
bones from his sack and called a tune.
Everyone watched and waited with bated
breath. Nothing happened. The pile of bones
didn't stir. The emperor grew restless, as did
everyone in the crowd. Kishi called another
tune and another. The bones remained at
rest. Kishi yelled and cursed at the bones
and began kicking them with his feet. Finally

the bones began to stir, moving slowly at first and then with deliberate speed. The skeleton assembled itself and stood up. The crowd gasped. The ruler leaned forward in his jeweled chair.

The skeleton walked up to His Majesty and bowed humbly before him. "My Lord and Protector, please hear me now. I've danced throughout Japan so that I might be brought before you. The man who calls the tunes killed and robbed me three years ago. He left me on a mountaintop to die alone. I was a good and honest man. I didn't deserve his cruelty."

So saying, the skeleton fell into a pile of bones, never to rise again.

The look of guilt on Kishi's face was enough to condemn him in the eyes of the court. He was taken to a cell and later put on trial for murder. Kishi was found guilty and sentenced to die.

## Wait Till Axel Comes

*United States*

A long time back, when haints and goblins came out to play on dark, lonely nights, an old, worn-out, broken-down preacher man came to an old, worn-out, broken-down house.

*This looks like a place for me,* he said to himself. *I wonder does anyone live here?*
"Anybody home?" he hollered loud. "I say there, anybody home?"

*"Meow . . . meow . . ."* came the answer from right behind the door.

"Meow your plain old self," said the preacher man, "and may the Good Lord bless and keep you. I'm coming in, Miss Meow, so don't go having a hissy-fit."

The old preacher man pushed the creaky, screechy door open and walked into the pitch-black room. "Lordy, Lordy, but it's dark in here, ain't it, Miss Meow? Where's my candle?"

Digging deep in his sermon sack, he came up with a stubby wax candle, burnt near to the bottom. He lit it with a wooden match and looked about the room. It was dusty and dirty. It was dank and dreary. It was full of broken furniture and glass.

"Now where's that cat gone to? Where are you, Miss Meow? You playing hide-and-seek with me? I'm good at hide-and-seek. I'll catch you up in no time. I'll get the fire going so I can see better, then I'll find your hidey-hole. Wait and see, just wait and see."

Logs were stacked next to the fireplace. Kindling was piled next to the logs. Old yellow newspapers were scattered about the filthy floor.

"Everything I need. Yes-in-deed-y, and I need everything."

He built the fire fine with the newspaper on the bottom, the kindling over that, and the logs on top. He touched the candle flame to the paper, and the fire burned bright. The flames danced high as the smoke flew right up the crumbling chimney. The room glowed bright.

*"Meow, meow."* It came from behind the closet door.

"So that's where you hid, you sneaky-sneak. Come out now and I'll give you a treat."

The closet door opened inch by inch. Two big yellow eyes peered out. "What kind of treat?" asked the cat. She stepped out of the closet and walked right up to the preacher man. She was the biggest, blackest cat he'd

ever seen. She licked his hand and asked,
"Will it taste better than you?"

"Oh Lord, protect me, protect me now,"
said the preacher man.

A second cat, larger than the first and just

as black, walked out of the closet. "Wait," said the second cat. "Don't eat him yet. We have to wait for Axel."

"Yes," said the third cat, coming from behind the closet door. He was bigger and blacker still. "We have to wait for Axel before we can eat."

"Who . . . who . . . who's Axel?" stammered the preacher man.

"Axel is Axel," said the first cat.

"And Axel does what Axel does," said the second.

"And what Axel does is tell us when to eat," said the third cat.

"We have to wait for Axel," said all three cats. "We have to wait for Axel."

The preacher man picked up his sermon-sack and took a big step back toward the broken-down door. "Tell Axel . . ." he said to the cats. He took another big step back toward the door. "Tell Axel that I . . ." A third step back. "Tell Axel that I couldn't . . ." One more step back and he was at the door. "Tell Axel that I couldn't wait!"

He turned and ran out of the broken-down house and down the dark night road in his broken-down shoes. And he never went back.

# The Hungry Witch

*Uruguay*

There was an evil and cruel witch who had lived for more than a thousand years. She knew many secrets. She could make plants and trees grow instantly. She could turn any living thing into another, such as a jaguar into a butterfly. She could fly in the daytime though not at night. And she was hungry. She was always hungry. She stole and ate cattle and goats from the villagers each night and awoke each morning with more hunger in her belly.

Brave warriors shot at her with arrows

and poison darts. They set clever traps and waited in the dark with heavy clubs. They sent messengers to her asking her to please leave them alone. Nothing worked. She couldn't be killed or tricked or begged. She was evil through and through, and she was always hungry.

In order to survive her hunger, farmers tied a fat cow, pig, or goat to a post outside the village at sundown each night. Everyone had to contribute. Families became poor, and the children grew thin.

One day, a brave youth with a good heart said, "The witch has too much power over us. We work too hard to feed her. I'm going into the forest, and when I find her, I'll kill her."

The village elders shook their heads and wrung their hands. "He's a foolish boy," they said. "Many strong youths have gone after her, but none have returned. He is doomed."

The lad walked deep into the forest. Before

night fell, he climbed into the branches of a
tall tree growing beside a deep lake. It wasn't
long before he heard the whisper of a scratchy
voice on the wind. It was the witch crooning to
the sleeping fish in the cold water below him:

*Come into my net, small fish and big fish.*
*Come into my net and fill up my dish.*
*This is my wish. This is my wish.*
*Tonight I'm hungry for fish.*

He watched in amazement as fish after
fish swam into her large net. After piling
them up on the lakeshore, she built a fire
and began roasting them. Delicious odors
floated up into the tree branches, prompting
the youth to lick his lips.

"I know you're up in the branches, lad.
I saw you the moment I arrived. You're
probably hungry, just like me. Come on
down and I'll share my feast."

The brave youth laughed loud. "I won't come down, and since its night, you can't fly up. I'll stay right here on this branch."

The witch made an ugly face and spoke a dark command to a small tree growing beside the youth's tree. Suddenly the small tree shot high into the air, its branches waving about. One of the branches knocked the boy out of his tree, and he plunged into the lake with a loud splash.

She cast her net into the lake once again, and its magic drew him in. He was caught. She carried him to her stone house, cackling, "You are young and strong. You'll make a good slave for many years to come." She dumped him in a small room and locked the door with a heavy lock.

Late the following day, a beautiful maiden arrived with food and drink. She had tears in her eyes.

"Who are you?" he asked.

"I'm the witch's slave," she said. "She caught me two years ago, but now that she has you, she'll eat me. That's what happened to the boy who was her slave before I arrived."

"Is there any way to escape?" he asked.

"She wears a magic green stone on the leather cord around her neck. It gives her the power to fly during the daytime. She carries a bag of magic powder in her apron pocket. It makes things grow and changes living things into other creatures. If we can take both stone and powder, perhaps we can escape."

The old witch came into the room. "What's taking so long, girl? I've started the fire, and it's time to roast you. Go climb into the pan."

Suddenly, the youth jumped up and grabbed the witch's hair with one hand and yanked the green stone from her neck with the other. She screamed and struggled with him. Before she could throw him against the wall, the maiden reached into the witch's apron pocket and snatched the bag of magic powder.

The boy put his arm around the girl, and with the green stone in hand, they rose into the air and out through the thatched roof. They flew into the late afternoon sky, high above the forest's treetops.

The witch wasn't defeated. She could run faster than any animal in the forest. She raced across the earth, keeping them in sight. She knew that the green stone wouldn't work after sunset. They would soon drift to the ground, and she would feast on both boy and girl. All the running was making her hungry.

As the sun began to set, the youth and maiden felt the tug of earth's gravity. The witch cackled far below. The girl sprinkled some of the magic powder into the air. It drifted down to the grass and turned each blade into a fat juicy rabbit. They jumped all about the witch's legs, and the temptation was too great. She stopped to eat a dozen hares.

The fleeing couple drifted closer to the earth. The witch caught up to them once again. The girl sprinkled more powder into the air, and it fell on a bush. The bush turned into a small deer. The witch couldn't help herself and stopped to feast again.

The sun was nearly gone beneath the horizon. The boy and girl drifted down near the lake where he first had been caught. Seeing them fall so close to the earth, the witch put on a great burst of speed. The pair drifted beyond the lakeshore and hovered just above the middle of the lake. The witch ran faster, her arms outstretched to catch them, and didn't stop in time. Running across the water to the deepest part, she began to sink.

"Help me! I can't swim! Help me!"

It was her only weakness, kept secret for a thousand years. Her head disappeared below the water, and she was gone.

The youth and maiden splashed down into the lake and swam quickly to shore. They returned home to his village where they were hailed as heroes. They were soon married and lived long and happy lives.

# The Cat on the Dovrefell

*Norway*

Long ago, a Norwegian named Orman found an orphaned polar bear cub in a winter cave. He took the cub home and raised it to a full-grown white bear. Traveling throughout the Norse land with the enormous and powerful bear at his side, Orman seldom met with trouble.

One snowy Christmas Eve, the man and bear began a journey to Denmark. They came to an inn on the Dovrefell and asked the proprietor, a fellow named Halvar, for a room.

"No rooms tonight," he said, "not for you

or your bear. You'll have to keep going."

"It's Christmas Eve," said Orman. "Where is your charity? You can't turn us out on Christmas Eve."

"I have no choice," said Halvar with a sigh. "I can't invite you to stay tonight of all nights. You wouldn't survive. No one would."

"What do you mean, not survive? There is little in this world that I fear, and the same can be said of my bear."

"It's the trolls," explained Halvor. "They come down from the mountain each Christmas Eve. They eat all our food, and drink all our drink. And they kill anyone who stays in the inn. My good wife and I prepare a feast for them and leave, just now, as the sun is setting."

"If it's trolls that worry you, then worry no more. My bear and I know how to deal with trolls."

As Halvor and his wife ran to safety in the

nearby village, Orman and his bear went inside the inn. The table in the main room lay heavy with scrumptious foods. Platters of ham and venison, bowls of carrots and onions, baskets of brown bread and rolls, pies and puddings, and a barrel of apple cider made a Christmas feast fit for the king himself.

"It all smells wonderful," said Orman, "but this isn't the time to eat. You curl up behind the warm stove, faithful bear, and I'll hide in the closet."

It wasn't long before the trolls tramped and stomped down the mountainside, chanting:

> *Time to eat, time to eat.*
> *Halvor's made our Christmas treat.*
> *You get the bread. I get the meat.*
> *Time to eat, time to eat.*

They were huge, ugly trolls with warts on their fat noses and green hair growing out of

their droopy ears. Entire troll families
arrived. There were old trolls and young
ones, fat trolls and thin ones. Seeing all the
food, they grunted and growled and slob-
bered on the floor. They were hungry!

Having no manners, the trolls didn't

bother to sit at the table. They grabbed at the food with filthy fingers and shoveled it in, not even taking the time to chew. They screamed at each other and gobbled and burped and belched. They broke the crockery and threw hard rolls and pudding at the walls.

One fat piece of venison slipped from a young troll's greasy hand and rolled behind the stove. He ran after it and, just as he grabbed it up, saw the bear lying there. "Here, little white cat," said the troll in a festive mood. "Do you want a bite?"

The polar bear growled and rose up to his full height. He roared with anger and cuffed the little troll across the room, landing him on his behind.

Taken by surprise, the rest of the trolls yelled with fright. They all ran from the inn and up the snowy mountainside, back to the safety of their cave.

Orman and his bear continued on their

journey early the next morning.

A year went by. It was Christmas Eve once again, and Halvor was outside his inn, drawing water from the well. He heard a strange voice from far away. It was the leader of the trolls calling down from the mountaintop.

"Innkeeper! Innkeeper! Do you still have that big white cat behind the stove?"

"Indeed I do," Halvor lied. "And she's had six big kittens who live with her still!"

"Then we can't come down for our Christmas feast tonight, not with all those white cats in your house."

The trolls never returned to Halvor's inn on the Dovrefell, not at Christmas nor ever again.

# The Ghost Wife

*Sioux*

In the time of long before, a young man learned to speak with animals. He often spent weeks at a time in the forest with his friends. Wolves, deer, bears, and birds of every size, color, and song kept him constant company.

One gentle summer afternoon, as he lay sleeping in a meadow, a tear rolled down his cheek. He was having a sad dream about the chief's beautiful daughter who had died from illness the week before. He had secretly loved the girl and felt that she, too, had cared for him. He wasn't a warrior, however, and hadn't been able to compete for her hand in marriage.

The dream ended, and the youth awoke. Sitting up, he cried out in alarm! Shimmering in the afternoon light, a beautiful and silent ghost stood before him. It was the chief's daughter.

*She's a spirit,* he thought. *She might harm me.*

Reading his thoughts, the ghost smiled and said, "Do not fear me. I've come because you are a special man. Return tomorrow if you wish. I'll talk further with you." So saying, she disappeared.

He went home to his village and told no one about the visitation. He returned to the meadow the following morning. When the ghost appeared, he told her the way of his heart. She was pleased. He built a small lodge to protect her from the wind and rain. He brought the buffalo robe from his lodge for her to sleep on. They stayed together for many moons.

One day he said to his spirit wife, "I've dreamed that my mother cries because I'm gone from the village. Please return with me to the people."

She thought for a long moment and answered, "Yes, I'll go with you, but only if you agree to these three things. Our lodge must be set apart from the others. I'll not visit with anyone in the daytime. You must never speak in anger to a child."

"I agree to each," he said happily.

The people were pleased when the young man returned with a new wife. His mother was happiest of all. He explained that she was from a small and distant tribe and had unusual ways of doing things.

"Do not be offended if she doesn't follow our ways," he said.

When the women of the tribe went to her lodge for a morning visit, they never found her home. When they returned in the evening with their husbands, the bride was extremely bashful. She served her guests with politeness but never spoke aloud. When asked a direct question, she smiled and let her husband answer. The people thought she was beautiful but strange indeed. After five new moons, they accepted her as one of the people.

The young husband and wife were happy for many seasons. A beautiful child was born to them on a cold winter night, and they raised the boy with gentleness and love.

One summer afternoon, the husband returned home from a long forest journey. Gone for many weeks, he'd grown accustomed to the calming sound of the wind in the trees. Birdsong still played in his ears. The gentle bubbling of the brook danced in his memory.

Now at home in his lodge, his hungry three-year-old son screamed and cried. Forgetting his long-held promise, the father yelled at his son to be quiet! There was anger in his voice.

His wife looked at him with horror and sadness. Grabbing her child's hand, they began to dissolve into the air.

"No!" cried the husband. "Please forgive me. I didn't mean it."

It was too late. The promise was broken. His ghost wife and their child were gone forever.

# Godfather Death

*Germany*

There once was a poor husband and wife who had seven hungry children. When the eighth was born, the man was desperate. He asked each of his neighbors to be the new boy's godfather.

"No, it's too much responsibility," they all said.

Thus the father said, "I'll ask the first stranger I see on the road to be the godfather."

He walked for a mile and came to a tall and beautiful man wearing a golden robe.

"Pardon me, stranger," said the new father,

"but I seek a godfather for my son."

"I'm no stranger," said the man in a deep and powerful voice. "I'm God. And yes, I'll be godfather to your son."

"Thank you, but no," said the man. "You give riches and happiness to some and poverty and bitterness to others. You don't play fairly. I can't let you be his godfather."

The man walked for another mile and came to a man dressed in black. He carried a silver cane and had a cruel face.

"I'm the Devil," he said in a sharp and chilling tone. "Let me be godfather to your son."

"Thank you, but no," said the father. "You tell lies and cheat honest people. I don't want you as his godfather."

A mile further down the road he came to a man as thin as a scarecrow. He wore a gray cloak and carried a large scythe. "I'm Death," he whispered in a cold voice. "I'll be your son's godfather."

"Thank you," said the man. "You treat everyone as equals. You'll make a fine godfather."

The child's christening was held the following day. Death appeared at the appointed hour and said all the proper words to confirm his role as godfather. He took the father aside after the ceremony and said, "From this day forth, you and your family will always have enough food to eat. On the day that my godchild turns eighteen, bring him to the place we met on the road. I'll give him a gift that will make him rich and famous."

Eighteen years later, the lad received his special gift. Death led him deep into the forest and showed him a rare herb growing at the base of a tree.

"Make tea with this herb and it will cure any disease. You'll become a famous doctor wherever you go. When you are called to a sick person's bed, you'll be able to see me. If

I'm standing at the head of the bed, the
person will live. Give the herbal tea and the
patient will soon recover. If I'm standing at
the foot of the bed, the patient belongs to
me. Simply say, 'There is no cure for this

one.' Never defy me, lad. Never try to change the outcome."

It wasn't long before the youth was known throughout the land as the doctor who was never wrong. He could tell if a person would recover or not with a single glance. He became rich as well as famous and lived happily for many years.

One day a summons came from the castle. The king had grown ill during the night. The doctor was ushered into the royal bedchamber and saw his godfather standing at the head of the bed. "The king will live," he announced. "I'll make a special tea, and he'll recover by tomorrow morning."

Everyone rejoiced, and indeed, the king was fit and fine the next day. He gave the doctor two large chests filled with gold and jewels and proclaimed him as the finest physician in the world.

A few months later, the king's only

daughter fell seriously ill. The doctor was immediately summoned and, upon arrival, saw Death standing at the foot of her bed.

"Save her," cried the king. "Save her as you did me."

Looking upon the elegant beauty of the sleeping princess, the doctor's heart cried out. He wanted to save her. *It isn't fair,* he thought. *I must try.*

Reaching down with both arms, he gently picked her up and reversed her position. Now her head rested at the foot of the bed. Godfather Death scowled at his godson and walked around to the head of the bed. The doctor picked up the princess a second time and returned her to her proper position. Death stood at her head. Shaking his head in anger, Death stalked out of the room.

The princess drank the healing tea and soon recovered. The king was so grateful that when the doctor asked if he could marry the princess, he readily agreed. The wedding date was set for the following week.

On the night before the wedding, Death visited his godson. He took him deep into the earth and showed him an enormous room filled with slow-burning candles.

"These are the flames that keep people alive," he explained. "That's why some of the candles are taller and some shorter. The shortest ones are the lives that will soon end." He pointed a long bony finger at a medium-sized candle. The flame flickered. "This is your light."

"Then I have half a life yet to live," said his godson.

"You did before you defied me," whispered Death. He blew on the flame, and the doctor's candle burned rapidly down to a stub.

"Please, Godfather, please!" cried the man. "Let me live."

Death slowly shook his head. The

flickering flame sputtered and went out. The doctor crumpled to the earth for he now belonged to Death.

The price of deceit is high, indeed, especially when paid in full.

# The Devil's Bridge

*France*

Hundreds of years ago, there was a small French mountain village built on the edge of a deep gorge. All travel beyond the village was made possible by a beautiful stone bridge arching over the gorge. The bridge was perfectly made. All the stones were cut and set by a master stonemason. Some said an angel made the bridge. Others said it was the Devil himself.

Whoever made it, the bridge was the pride of all the villagers. They used it each week to lead cattle to market and to return

home again, carrying new pots, tools, sewing thread, and fresh vegetables.

One terrible night, a thunderstorm rolled down the mountainside, bringing calamity in its wake. Lightning struck buildings, setting them ablaze; thunder boomed so loud that children and their parents hid under their beds. Ancient trees were uprooted, and entire rooftops were sent flying through the air. Then it happened: a lightning bolt smashed into the center of the bridge's arch. A great rumble and roar followed as the entire bridge collapsed into the deep gorge.

The storm soon ended. The first rays of morning light shone down on the pile of stones at the bottom of the gorge. The villagers wept.

"How will I get my cattle to market?" wailed one man.

"How will I visit my sick mother in the next village?" cried a woman. "We're not mountain climbers. We can't slide to the bottom of the gorge and climb back up the other, steep side."

"I have three dozen eggs to sell at the fair in the next town," said another woman. "The fair ends this afternoon. All is lost."

"We must build another bridge, and that's all there is to it," said one of the men. "Old Jacques is our stonemason."

Old Jacques, bent with age and ill health, stepped to the edge of the gorge and looked down. He shook his head and said, "It's too big a job and I'm too old. Even in my youth it would have taken ten skilled masons a year or more to build such a bridge."

The villagers sighed with disappointment.

Suddenly, a stranger appeared among them. He wore a long black coat, a top hat, and odd-looking boots. His eyes shone gray, then yellow, then black. Perhaps it was the morning light. The people backed away. Village dogs and cats ran to hide.

"You seem to have a problem," the stranger said in a rich but dark voice. "You need a new bridge, and I'm just the man to do it. I'm an expert at bridge building, even if I do say so myself. I'd be pleased to help you out."

One of the village elders asked, "What is your fee? We have little gold in the town coffers."

The stranger doffed his top hat, exposing sharp horns growing from his head. The villagers gasped and took another step back. "Have no fear," he said. "I'm not here to harm you. I've come to build a bridge. I have no need of gold, but I do need a fresh soul. Let's strike a bargain: the bridge for a soul. I'll take the soul of the first to cross the bridge once it's finished. What say you?"

After much hemming and hawing, after much arguing and shouting, after much pleading and weeping, the villagers agreed: the bridge for a soul.

The bargain made, the Devil went to work. Speaking in Latin, he recited a long series of evil-sounding words. Suddenly there was a thunderclap and a flash of light. The bottom of the gorge opened up, and a thousand lost souls rushed out to do the Devil's work. They sorted the stones and lay them in place, one by one, faster and faster, until it was done. The perfect new bridge arched the gorge once again. The lost souls, swallowed up by the hole in the earth, were gone.

"Ah yes," said the Devil. "It's time for my payment. Who will be first to cross the bridge?"

The villagers stammered and shook and tried to hide behind each other. No one noticed that Old Jacques had quietly slipped away from the crowd. No one noticed that he started climbing down the bridge pilings on the village side. No one noticed that when he reached the bottom of the gorge, he crossed it and then began pulling himself up the bridge pilings on the other side. He was old, but his arms were strong from all the rocks he carried as a younger man. Once he was on the other side of the bridge, however, everyone noticed him.

"Mr. Devil!" he yelled. "Look over here."

The Devil and everyone in the crowd looked, just as Old Jacques began ringing a cowbell and waving a large handful of sweet hay in the air. Suddenly, an old milk cow broke from the crowd and began running across the bridge. It was his favorite cow, near the end of her life and accustomed to the sound of the bell announcing her dinnertime. She made it all the way across and was rewarded with a hug around the neck and a mouthful of sweet hay.

"There you have it," yelled Old Jacques. "The soul of my cow, as she was the first to cross the bridge."

The Devil stormed across the bridge, yelling, "I don't want the soul of a cow; I want a person. You knew I wanted a person."

"Yes," agreed Old Jacques, "but you didn't say that in the terms of the bargain. You said 'the soul of the first to cross the bridge.' So you must take the soul of my cow."

The Devil knew the rules as well as anyone. He'd been tricked and defeated fairly. Spitting out the words, he said, "I'll remember you, Old Jacques. Your time is short here on earth, and if your soul is dark, it's mine. Then I'll have my revenge."

With a puff of black smoke, the Devil disappeared.

The villagers rushed across the wonderful bridge and cheered for their hero. Old Jacques just smiled, knowing that indeed, his time on earth was short. Since it was an angel who had whispered in his ear, giving him the idea for the cow to cross first, he knew that he wouldn't meet up with the Devil ever again.

# The Horned Women

*Ireland*

The woman of the house stayed up late into the night carding wool. Her three wee children were fast asleep in the back room. The wind blew hard against the windows and door. "Did someone knock?" she asked the black cat resting by her feet.

The cat licked her forepaw. The wind continued to howl. The woman heard it again, a tapping at her door. "It must be Neighbor Sally come to ask for milk."

She got up from her chair by the fire and opened the door against the heavy wind. It wasn't Neighbor Sally standing there with an empty cup. It was an old witch-woman with a sharp horn growing from her forehead.

The witch pushed her way into the room and sat down in the woman's chair. She picked up the wool carder and set to work, saying, "Where are my sisters? They should be here by now."

Along with the night wind there came another knocking at the door. The house woman slowly opened it. A witch with two horns growing from her forehead carried a spinning wheel inside. She placed it next to the fire and began to spin the carded wool.

The house woman began to protest. "Now see here, good woman, this is not . . ." and her mouth closed tight. The witches placed a spell of silence upon her for the remainder of the night. The door opened and closed, opened and closed, a total of ten times more. Ten more witches arrived, each with one

more horn growing from her head. Twelve
horns covered the head of the last witch, as
she was the oldest of all. They carded and
spun the wool, weaving it into a beautiful
cloak, until the break of day.

"We're hungry, woman," said the witch with
five horns. "Make us a breakfast cake. Fetch
the well water in a sieve to make it right."

The frightened house woman took the
sieve to the well. She dipped it in, and all the
water poured back out. She began to cry.

A voice, pure and sweet, rose from the well.
"Seal the holes with clay from the earth and

moss from the trees." It was the spirit of the well who watched over the farm and family.

The spell of silence dissolved with the rising of the sun, and the woman had her voice back. She explained what had happened and asked for help. The spirit told her how to make the witches leave.

The woman lined the sieve with moss and plastered over all the tiny holes with clay. She carried the sieve of water back into the house. The witches looked at each other with suspicion. Who had told her the secret?

They mixed the well water with flour and a drop of blood taken from each of the sleeping children, and placed the cake on the fire.

Immediately the house woman ran to the north corner of the room, yelling:

*The witch's mountain is burning down!*
*The witch's mountain is burning down!*
*The witch's mountain is burning down!*

The twelve horned women screamed as one and ran out of the house, away to their sacred mountain.

The spirit of the well spoke again to the woman. "The evil ones will return tonight. You must protect your family. Listen carefully."

The house woman washed her children's feet in clean well water. She then sprinkled the water on the ground outside her door. Scooping up the cake made of flour, water, and blood, she made each child eat one bite. She gathered up the long woolen cloak and locked it in a stout chest. Finally, she barred the door with a heavy log.

Night fell fast and hard. A dark wind began to blow. The witches arrived all in a rage, stamping their ugly feet on the ground.

"Feet-water, let us in! Don't keep us out. Don't keep us out!"

"You'll not trespass over me," spoke the feet-water. "You'll not trespass over me."

"Open door, open now!" cried the horned women.

"Never," said the door log. "You can't come in."

"Blood-cake, you belong to us. Open the door and let us in!"

"I cannot," spoke the cake. "I'm broken into pieces, and the children have taken a bite. I have no more power."

"Woolen cloak, you are strong. Open this door and let us in," they pleaded.

"I'm locked in the woman's chest," said the cloak. "Now I belong to her. Your spell is broken in this house, now and forever."

Screaming curses at the house and its pro-tectors, the twelve horned women ran off into the night.

The woman kept the witches' cloak locked in her chest for years and years. The only time she opened the lid to let others peek in was at the end of the story she told, the very same story I've just told to you.

# The Talking Skull

*Congo*

Long ago, at the edge of a thirsty forest, a simple hunter named Kwame searched for food. He was hungry. His family was hungry. His entire *kraal* (village) was hungry. The rain hadn't fallen in three years; a drought was on the land. Kwame found a tall, lonely tree and knelt down to peek into its exposed roots. An ancient skull lay hidden there. A cold shiver rushed up his spine.

"I'm hungry, old skull. Can you point me in the direction of food?" asked the hunter. He was joking, but speaking aloud calmed

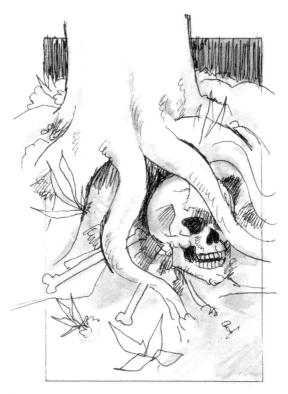

his fears.

Suddenly, the skull's lower jaw moved up and down. "Yes," it said, "but why should I help you?"

Kwame screamed and leapt back, startling several small birds, hidden in the tree's branches, into flight. "Oh my," said the hunter. "I must be dreaming. I thought the skull spoke to me. A skull can't talk. Everyone knows that."

"Then everyone is wrong," said the skull. "I can talk. I'm talking to you. Do you want my help or not?"

"Ye-ye-yesss," stammered Kwame. "Everyone in my *kraal* is starving. The lack of rain has made our crops fail again and again. We need food or we will die. Please help me if you can."

"You are brave and speak with respect," said the skull. "These are qualities I like. I'll help you find food, but on one condition. You must promise to never tell another about me."

"I promise," replied Kwame.

"Follow the trail that leads east from here. You'll soon find a special field of small pumpkins. Take only what you can carry in your hunter's sack. Tell no one else about me or the field."

"Thank you, oh mighty skull." Kwame ran east on the trail and found the pumpkin patch. He quickly filled his sack and ran back to his *kraal*. Kwame was called a hero, and everyone enjoyed a pumpkin feast that night. The villagers were hungry again the following day.

Kwame returned to the lonely tree at the forest's edge and spoke to the skull. "Is it proper for me to take a sack of pumpkins each day until the drought ends?"

"Since you ask permission, I say yes. Remember, tell no one about me or the field."

"I'll remember, friend skull. I'm curious. How did your life end so long ago?"

"I was killed because of my tongue."

"Your tongue? How did your tongue get you killed?"

"You ask too many questions, hunter. Gather your pumpkins and leave me alone."

Kwame brought food to his *kraal* each day for several weeks. One night the rains fell, ending the drought. A celebration feast was planned.

"Tell me, Kwame," said the chief. "How did you find the field of pumpkins?"

The chief was powerful. He had to be given an answer.

"A friend told me about it," said Kwame.

"Who is this friend?"

"I can't tell you, oh Great Chief. I'd like to, but I made a promise."

"You will tell me or suffer the consequences," demanded the chief.

Kwame knew that the consequences would be extremely painful, as the chief always got what he wanted. "It was a talking skull," he said. "I found it at the edge of the forest."

"I'd like to have a skull that can talk," said the chief. "It will frighten my enemies. Bring it to me. I'll send three of my warriors with you. Do not fail me."

The warriors followed Kwame to the tree

and made him dig the skull out from in-between the roots.

"I'm sorry, skull, but my chief makes me do this. Please don't be angry with me."

The skull said nothing.

Back at the *kraal*, the chief held the skull in his large hand and said, "Talk to me, skull. Tell me why you helped this village."

The skull didn't answer.

"I'm the chief. I demand that you talk to me."

The skull remained silent.

"No one makes a fool of me and lives to tell of it," shouted the chief. "Take this old skull back to the tree where you found it. Take Kwame with you and end his life. I have spoken."

Kwame was dragged back to the lonely tree and tied to its exposed roots. The skull was set beside him. Just before death came, the skull whispered, "You see? Just as my tongue killed me, so did your tongue kill you."

# Notes

The stories in this collection are my retellings of tales from throughout the world. They have come to me from written and oral sources and result from thirty years of my telling them aloud.

None of the nine tales herein have been included in my previous collections. Motifs given are from *The Storyteller's Sourcebook: A Subject, Title and Motif Index to Folklore Collections for Children* by Margaret Read MacDonald (Detroit: Neal–Schuman/Gale, 1982); and *The Storyteller's Sourcebook: A Subject, Title and Motif Index to Folklore Collections for Children 1983–1999* by Margaret Read MacDonald and Brian W. Sturm (Detroit: Gale Group, 2001).

### The Dancing Skeleton — Japan

Motif E632.1. This basic plot of revenge and justice is found throughout the world. It has been recorded in China, Germany, Africa, and the United States. My initial encounter with this story was in the departure area of Tokyo's International Airport in the fall of 2001. My London flight was delayed, and a Japanese middle school teacher and I passed the time sharing stories.

Variants are found in *Folktales of Japan* by Keigo Seki (Chicago: University of Chicago Press, 1963), pp. 145–148; and *World Folktales* by Anita Stern (Lincolnwood, Illinois: National Textbook Company, 1994), pp. 145–149.

### Wait Till Axel Comes — United States

Motif J1495.2. Also known as "Wait Till Martin Comes," this is a classic tale from the American South. I first heard it during a Halloween celebration while in the third grade. Slowly build the tension until the preacher man finally flees. Then run (imaginatively and vocally) as if Axel has already arrived. It usually brings a laugh of relief.

For other variants see *The Thing at the Foot of the Bed and Other Scary Tales* by Maria Leach (Cleveland: World, 1959), pp. 23–26; and *Ghosts and Goblins: Stories for Halloween* by Wilhelmina Harper (New York: Dutton, 1936, 1964), pp. 195–198.

### The Hungry Witch — Uruguay

Motif G530.2N. This South American variant of "Hansel and Gretel" is fun to tell because the witch is insatiably hungry. It contains the essential ingredients of a powerful story experience for young listeners: evil, courage, magic, and accomplishment.

Two variants are found in *Tales From Silver Lands* by Charles J. Finger (Garden City, New York:

Doubleday, 1924), pp. 135–145; and *A Baker's Dozen: Thirteen Stories to Tell and Read Aloud* by Mary Gould Davis (New York: Harcourt, 1930), pp. 1–20.

### The Cat on the Dovrefell — Norway

Motif K1728. The Dovrefell is a plateau, 7,565 feet in elevation, in central Norway. This popular Scandinavian Christmas story succeeds in the telling with proper emphasis placed on the horrible, hungry, ugly trolls. Have fun.

Variants are found in *East of the Sun and West of the Moon* by Peter Christian Asbjørnsen and Jørgen Moe Asbjørnsen (New York: Macmillan, 1953), pp. 125–127; and *Scandinavian Stories* by Margaret Sperry (New York: Watts, 1971), pp. 29–37.

### The Ghost Wife — Sioux

Motif E474.5. The spirit world comes alive in the Sioux's rich story culture. This delicate and ultimately sad story adds balance to a program of scary tales. It was initially collected and retold in *Wigwam Evenings: Sioux Folk Tales Retold* by Charles A. Goodman and Elaine Goodale Eastman (Boston: Little Brown, 1909), pp. 245–253. It's also found in *Ghosts and Goblins: Stories for Halloween* by Wilhelmina Harper (New York: Dutton, 1936, 1964), pp. 99–102.

### Godfather Death — Germany

Motif D1825.3.1.1.1. Based on oral sources and adapted from European medieval literary tomes, this is another of the Grimm Brothers' tales that deserves to be read and told for centuries to come. In various adaptations, Death is tricked and leaves in anger, allowing the doctor to live. I prefer the original ending.

See *The Brothers Grimm: Popular Folk Tales* by Jakob Ludwig Karl Grimm and Wilhelm Grimm (Garden City, New York: Doubleday, 1978), pp. 97–101. A Swedish version is found in *One Hundred Favorite Folktales* by Stith Thompson (Bloomington, Indiana: Indiana University Press, 1968), pp. 73–76.

### The Devil's Bridge — France

Motif S241.1. Depending upon the adaptation of this popular European tale, it might be a cat, dog, goat, or the Devil himself who crosses the bridge first. I first heard the "cow" version from a French graduate student at the University of Massachusetts in Amherst, in 1968.

Another variant is found in *Welsh Legendary Tales* by Elisabeth Sheppard-Jones (Edinburgh: Nelson, 1959), pp. 173–177. See also *Round About and Long Ago: Tales from the English Counties* by Eileen Colwell (Boston: Houghton Mifflin, 1972), pp 23–26.

### The Horned Women — Ireland

Motif F381.8.1. The concept of "feet-water" as a protection against evil is purely Irish. My initial encounter with this intriguing tale was as a high school senior in the Denver Public Library. I liked old stories, and for a book report, my English teacher suggested I read a collection by Joseph Jacobs. I discovered it in *Celtic Folk and Fairy Tales* by Joseph Jacobs (New York: Putnam, n.d.), pp. 34–37.

Another source is *The Talking Tree* by Augusta Baker (Philadelphia: Lippincott, 1955), pp. 48–51.

### The Talking Skull — Congo

Motif B210.2.3. I first heard this story while teaching at the College of the Virgin Islands in St. Thomas, during the summer of 1967. The assignment was to share an old story still told in one's family. Many of the stories originated in Africa.

A variant is found in *African Genesis* by Leo Frobenius and Douglas C. Fox (New York: Benjamin Blom, 1937, 1966), pp. 161–162. Another variant is found in *The Thing at the Foot of the Bed and Other Scary Tales* by Maria Leach (Cleveland: World, 1959), pp. 49–50.